MW01635871

PET PARTY

Hal O. Graham

Holo Popups
Baltimore, Maryland

PET PARTY

How to use **Holo Popups**:

Follow these steps to bring these pages to life!

-Download the **Holo Popups** AR App from the App Store or Google Play.

-Turn on your sound and open the **Holo Popups** AR App.

-Point the spinning cursor at the pages with images.

-Watch as the pages are transformed into beautiful 3D animations.

-Save your photos & videos and share with your friends & family!

Having trouble? Here are a few things to try:

-Make sure the full image is in view (hold the phone 1-2 feet from the page).

-Flatten the pages if tracking is jumpy.

-Turn on the flash ⚡ in low lighting.

Email us at support@baltivirtual.com for help!

Enjoy the magic of **Holo Popups!**

People have had pet goldfish
for over a thousand years!
They've been around a long time,
much longer than their pet peers.

Goldfish have long memories,
much longer than you've heard.
You can even teach them tricks,
and they can recognize words.

This little Bulldog puppy
has a great big heavy head.
It's great for pats and scratches
when he curls up on your bed.

Bulldogs were bred for hunting
and for herding bulls around.
These days, they're college mascots,
helping their teams score touchdowns!

This cat is playing with yarn,
batting it all over the floor.
She'll unravel it if she's not careful,
and make a mess you can't ignore.

Cats love to chase and play with toys -
it's how they learn to hunt.
So when she runs after a laser pointer,
it's not just an adorable stunt!

These two bunnies are playing together,
chasing each other in the grass.
Maybe they'll share some plants for lunch -
hopefully, they won't eat too fast!

Bunnies also make great family pets!
They're easy to housebreak and train.
You can teach bunnies to do funny tricks
and respond when you call their name.

Look at this handsome tomcat!
He's got stripes all over his fur.
If you tickle him under his chin,
he'll roll on his back and purr.

He can jump up to seven times his own height,
and he'll chase mice and rats away.
But good luck waking him up from his naps -
he sleeps 18 hours a day!

This guy's called a 'yellow tang,'
and he's tropical and fun!
A lot of pet stores have them,
so it's easy to get one.

Yellow tangs like saltwater,
and seaweed's their favorite food.
Have enough of that around,
and they'll be in a great mood!

Bunnies love to run and hop,
and boy, they're as cute as can be!
With their cotton ball tails and floppy ears,
one look at them and you'll agree.

The name for a lady rabbit is “doe,”
and a boy rabbit is called a “buck.”
The name for baby rabbits is “kits,”
and there are lots of them running amok!

This pretty spotted dog
is known as a Dalmatian.
Her smooth coat and friendly face
make her quite a sensation!

You've probably seen Dalmatians
on the backs of fire trucks.
Firemen use Dalmatians
both as guard dogs and good luck!

Golden Retrievers are popular dogs!
They're some of the smartest ones, too.
If you throw a stick or a ball,
this puppy can bring it right back to you.

Golden puppies are helpful
and really like making new friends.
So if you've got a bunny or cat, or a fish,
they'll be its best friend to the end!

Another friendly puppy!
This one's wagging her tail.
That means she's glad to see you.
Scratch behind her ears - you can't fail!

Make sure to pet this puppy a lot,
and now's a good time to start.
It'll make her happy, and plus,
petting dogs is good for your heart!

Holo Popups is a publisher focused on augmented reality children's books. By bringing the best authors and the best animators together, we seek to create a uniquely magical experience for your child. Images on the pages come alive to entertain, educate, and energize your child. Books in the series appeal to a range of interests. They can be a part of your parent-child reading/bonding time as well as a cool, motivational tool for children to learn on their own.

Hal O. Graham was born and raised in Baltimore, Maryland. He spent his childhood reading pop-up books and has now moved on to developing augmented reality children's books. Hal wants your child's joy for reading to come to life just like the animations in his books. Hal loves science fiction, magic, and illusions. When not working on his latest children's book, Hal can be found hanging out with his virtual friends, created by the team at Holo Popups.

Made in the USA
San Bernardino, CA
24 November 2018